Text copyright © 2015 by Harriet Ziefert
Illustrations copyright © 2015 by Elliot Kreloff
All rights reserved / CIP date is available.
Published in the United States by
🍎 Blue Apple Books
515 Valley Street, Maplewood, NJ 07040
www.blueapplebooks.com

First Edition
Printed in China 02/15
Hardcover ISBN: 978-1-60905-510-3
Paperback ISBN: 978-1-60905-578-3
1 3 5 7 9 10 8 6 4 2

10
Little Fish

10
Pececitos

by **Harriet Ziefert**

illustrations by **Elliot Kreloff**

BLUE APPLE

Yellow fish, blue fish,

Pez amarillo, pez azul,

We count **TWO** fish.

Contamos **DOS** peces.

THREE fish,
TRES peces,

FOUR fish,
We see more fish.

CUATRO peces,
Vemos más peces.

Swim and dive fish.

Peces que nadan y saltan.

Here are
FIVE fish.

Aquí hay
CINCO peces.

Short fish,
Peces cortos,

Long fish,
Peces largos,

SIX
swim-along fish.

SEIS
peces nadando.

Fish above,
Peces arriba,

fish below.
peces abajo.

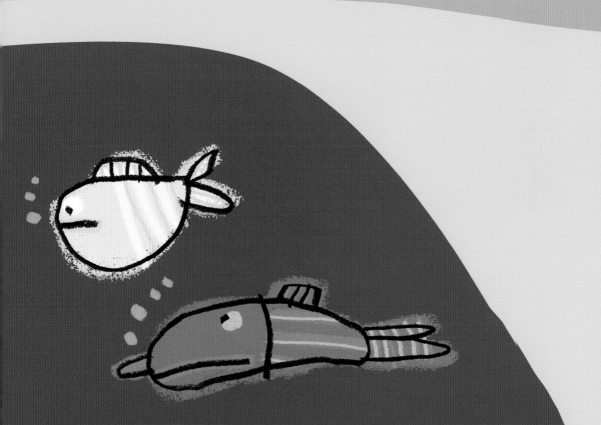

SEVEN fish, fast and slow.

SIETE peces, rápidos y lentos.

Wiggly fish,
Peces meneándose,

Straight fish,
Peces rectos,

We count
EIGHT fish.

Contamos
OCHO peces.

**Spotted fish,
striped fish.**

Peces manchados,
peces rayados.

NINE fish swim and swish.

NUEVE peces nadan y chapotean.

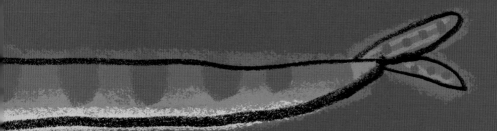

Big fish,
Peces grandes,
small fish.
peces pequeños.

TEN in all fish.
Son **DIEZ** peces en total.

10 - 9 - 8 - 7- 6

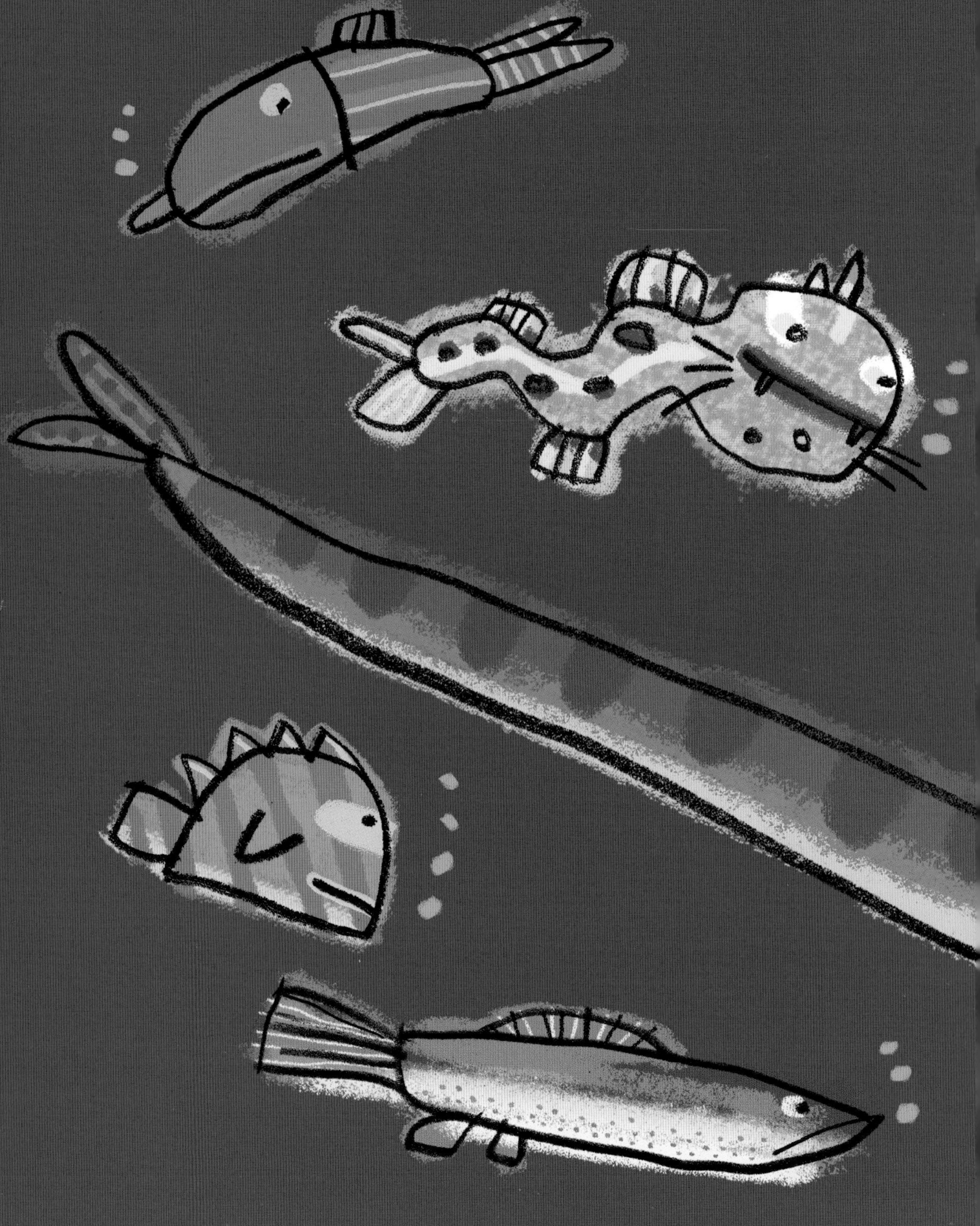

Ready or not . . .
Listos o no . . .

Here we come!
Ya vamos!